Rennell Rodd

Songs in the South

Rennell Rodd

Songs in the South

ISBN/EAN: 9783744772525

Printed in Europe, USA, Canada, Australia, Japan

Cover: Foto ©Andreas Hilbeck / pixelio.de

More available books at **www.hansebooks.com**

SONGS IN THE SOUTH

BY

RENNELL RODD

LONDON

DAVID BOGUE

3, St. Martin's Place, Trafalgar Square

1881

CHISWICK PRESS :—C. WHITTINGHAM AND CO., TOOKS COURT,
CHANCERY LANE.

TO

MY FATHER.

CHISWICK PRESS :—C. WHITTINGHAM AND CO., TOOKS COURT,
CHANCERY LANE.

TO

MY FATHER.

CONTENTS.

SONGS IN THE SOUTH.

SONNETS.

SONGS.

8   *CONTENTS.*

SONGS IN THE SOUTH.

FROM THE HILL OF GARDENS.

THE outline of a shadowy city spread
 Between the garden and the distant hill—
And o'er yon dome the flame-ring lingers still,
Set like the glory on an angel's head :
The light fades quivering into evening blue
Behind the pine-tops on Ianiculum ;
The swallow whispered to the swallow "come !"
And took the sunset on her wings, and flew.

One rift of cloud the wind caught up suspending
A ruby path between the earth and sky ;
Those shreds of gold are angel wings ascending
From where the sorrows of our singers lie ;
They have not found those wandering spirits yet,
But seek for ever in the red sunset.

Pass upward angel wings ! Seek not for these,
They sit not in the cypress-planted graves ;
Their spirits wander over moonlit waves,
And sing in all the singing of the seas ;

And by green places in the spring-tide showers,
And in the re-awakening of flowers.

Some pearl-lipped shell still dewy with sea foam
Bear back to whisper where their feet have trod ;
They are the earth's for ever more ; fly home !
And lay a daisy at the feet of God.   .

IN THE COLISEUM.

NIGHT wanes ; I sit in the ruin alone ;
　　Beneath, the shadow of arches falls
From the dim outline of the broken walls ;
And the half-light steals o'er the age-worn stone
From a midway arch where the moon looks through,
　　A silver shield in the deep deep blue.

This is the hour of ghosts that rise ;
—Line on line of the noiseless dead—
The clouds above are their awning spread ;
Look into the shadow with moon-dazed eyes,
You will see the writhing of limbs in pain,
　　And the whole red tragedy over again.

The ghostly galleys ride out and meet,
　The Cæsar sits in his golden chair,
His fingers toy with his women's hair,
The water is blood-red under his feet,—
Till the owl's long cry dies down with the night,
　　And one star waits for the dawning light.

Rome, 1881.

AT TIBER MOUTH.

THE low plains stretch to the west with a glimmer of
    rustling weeds,
Where the waves of a golden river wind home by the
    marshy meads ;
And the strong wind born of the sea grows faint with a
    sickly breath,
As it stays in the fretting rushes and blows on the dews
    of death.
We came to the silent city, in the glare of the noontide heat,
When the sound of a whisper rang through the length of
    the lonely street ;
No tree in the clefted ruin, no echo of song nor sound,
But the dust of a world forgotten lay under the barren
    ground.
There are shrines under these green hillocks to the beau-
    tiful gods that sleep,
Where they prayed in the stormy season for lives gone
    out on the deep ;
And here in the grave street sculptured, old record of
    loves and tears,

By the dust of the nameless slave, forgotten a thousand
years.
Not ever again at even shall ship sail in on the breeze,
Where the hulls of their gilded galleys came home from a
hundred seas,
For the marsh plants grow in her haven, the marsh birds
breed in her bay,
And a mile to the shoreless westward the water has
passed away.
But the sea-folk gathering rushes come up from the
windy shore,
So the song that the years have silenced grows musical
there once more ;
And now and again unburied, like some still voice from
the dead,
They light on the fallen shoulder and the lines of a
marble head.
But we went from the sorrowful city and wandered away
at will,
And thought of the breathing marble and the words that
are music still.
How full were their lives that laboured, in their fetterless
strength and far
From the ways that our feet have chosen as the sunlight
is from the star,
They clung to the chance and promise that once while
the years are free

Look over our life's horizon as the sun looks over the sea,
But we wait for a day that dawns not, and cry for un-
    clouded skies,
And while we are deep in dreaming the light that was
    o'er us dies ;
We know not what of the present we shall stretch out our
    hand to save
Who sing of the life we long for, and not of the life we
    have ;
And yet if the chance were with us to gather the days
    misspent,
Should we change the old resting-places, the wandering
    ways we went ?
They were strong, but the years are stronger; they are
    grown but a name that thrills,
And the wreck of their marble glory lies ghost-like over
    their hills.
So a shadow fell o'er our dreaming for the weary heart of
    the past,
For the seed that the years have scattered, to reap so
    little at last.

And we went to the sea-shore forest, through a long
    colonnade of pines,
Where the skies peep in and the sea, with a flitting of
    silver lines.

And we came on an open place in the green deep heart of
    the wood
Where I think in the years forgotten an altar of Faunus
    stood ;
From a spring in the long dark grasses two rivulets rise
    and run
By the length of their sandy borders where the snake lies
    coiled in the sun.
And the stars of the white narcissus lie over the grass
    like snow,
And beyond in the shadowy places the crimson cyclamens
    grow ;
Far up from their wave home yonder the sea-winds mur-
    muring pass,
The branches quiver and creak and the lizard starts in
    the grass.
And we lay in the untrod moss and pillowed our cheeks
    with flowers,
While the sun went over our heads, and we took no count
    of the hours ;
From the end of the waving branches and under the
    cloudless blue
Like sunbeams chained for a banner the threadlike gos-
    samers flew.
And the joy of the woods came o'er us and we felt that
    our world was young
With the gladness of years unspent and the sorrow of life
    unsung.

So we passed with a sound of singing along to the sea-
        ward way,
Where the sails of the fishermen folk came homeward
        over the bay ;
For a cloud grew over the forest and darkened the sea-
        god's shrine,
And the hills of the silent city were only a ruby line.
But the sun stood still on the waves as we passed from the
        fading shores,
And shone on our boat's red bulwarks and the golden
        blades of the oars,
And it seemed as we steered for the sunset that we
        passed through a twilight sea,
From the gloom of a world forgotten to the light of a
        world to be.

    Rome, 1881.

A ROMAN MIRROR.

THEY found it in her hollow marble bed,
　　There where the numberless dead cities sleep,
　They found it lying where the spade struck deep,
A broken mirror by a maiden dead.

These things—the beads she wore about her throat
　　Alternate blue and amber all untied,
　A lamp to light her way, and on one side
The toll men pay to that strange ferry-boat.

No trace to-day of what in her was fair !
　　Only the record of long years grown green
　Upon the mirror's lustreless dead sheen,
Grown dim at last, when all else withered there.

Dead, broken, lustreless ! It keeps for me
　　One picture of that immemorial land,
　For oft as I have held thee in my hand
The dull bronze brightens, and I dream to see

A fair face gazing in thee wondering wise,
   And o'er one marble shoulder all the while
   Strange lips that whisper till her own lips smile,
And all the mirror laughs about her eyes.

It was well thought to set thee there, so she
   Might smooth the windy ripples of her hair
   And knot their tangled waywardness, or ere
She stood before the queen Persephone.

And still it may be where the dead folk rest,
   She holds a shadowy mirror to her eyes,
   And looks upon the changelessness, and sighs
And sets the dead land lilies in her breast.

1879.

•

BY THE SOUTH SEA.

SO here we have sat by the sea so late,
  And you with your dreaming eyes
Have argued well what I know you hate,
  Till even my own dream dies.

Yet why will you smile at my old white years
  When love was a gift divine,
When songs were laughter and hope and tears,
  And art was a people's shrine?

Must I change the burdens I loved to sing,
  The words of my worn-out song?
The old fair thoughts have a hollow ring,
  My faiths have been dead so long.

And yet,—to have known that one did not know !
  To have dreamed with the poet priest !
To have hope to feel that it might be so !
  And theirs was a faith at least,

When the priest was poet, and hearts were fain
  Of marvellous things to dream,
To see God's tears in a cloud of rain,
  And his hair on a gold sunbeam ;

To know that the sons of the old Sea King
  Roamed under their waves at will,
To have heard a song that the wood gods sing
  On the other side of the hill !

And so I had held it,—for all things blend
  In the world's great harmony,—
That they served an end to an after-end,
  And were of the things that be.

But now ye are bidding *your* God god-speed
  With his lore upon dusty shelves ;
So wise ye are grown, ye have found no need
  For any god but yourselves.

Ye have learnt the riddle of seas and sand,
  Of leaves in the spring uncurled ;
There is no room left for my wonderland
  In the whole of the great wide world.

And what have ye left for a song to say?
  What now is a singer's fame ?
He may startle the ear with a word one day,
  And die,—and live in a name.

But the world has heed unto no fair thing,
  Men pass on their soulless ways,
They give no faith unto those who sing,
  —Give hardly a heartless praise.

But you say, Let us go unto all wide lands,
  Let us speak to the people's heart !
Let us make good use of our lips and hands,
  There is hope for the world in art !

Will the dull ears hear, will the dead souls see ?
  Will they know what we hardly know ?
The chords of the wonderful harmony
  Of the earth and the skies ?—if so—

We have talked too long till it all seems vain,—
  The desire and the hopes that fired,
The triumphs won and the meedless pain,
  And the heart that has hoped is tired.

Do you see down there where the high cliffs shrink,
  And the ripples break on the bay,
Our old sea boat at the white foam brink
  With the sail slackened down half-way ?

Shall we get hence ? O fair heart's brother !
  You are weary at heart with me,
We two alone in the world, no other :
  Shall we go to our wide kind sea ?

Shall we glide away in this white moon's track ?
  Does it not seem fair in your eyes !
—To drift and drift with our white sail black
  In the dreamful light of the skies,

Till the pale stars die, and some far fair shore
  Comes up through the morning haze,
And wandering hearts shall not wander more
  Far off from the mad world's ways.

Or still more fair—when the dim scared night
  Grows pale from the east to the west—
If the waters gather us home, and the light
  Break through on the waves' unrest,

And there in the gleam of the gold-washed sea,
  Which the smile of the morning brings,
Our souls shall fathom the mystery,
  And the riddle of all these things.

1879.

IN A CHURCH.

THIS was the first shrine lit for Queen Marie ;
    And I will sit a little at her feet,
For winds without howl down the narrow street
And storm-clouds gather from the westward sea.

Sweet here to watch the peasant people pray,
    While through the crimson-shrouded window falls
    Low light of even, and the golden walls
Grow dim and dreamful at the end of day,

Till from these columns fades their marble sheen,
    And lines grow soft and mystical,—these wraiths
    That watch the service of the changing faiths,
To Mary mother from the Cyprian queen.

But aye for me this old-world colonnade
    Seems open to blue summer skies once more,
    These altars pass, and on the polished floor
I see the lines of chequered light and shade ;

I seem to see the dark-browed Lybian lean
   To cool the tortured burning of the lash,
   I see the fountains as they leap and flash,
The rustling sway of cypress set between.

And now yon friar with the bare feet there,
   Is grown the haunting spirit of the place ;
   Ah ! brown-robed friar with the shaven face,
The saints are weary of thy mumbled prayer.

From matins' bell to the slow day's decline
   He sits and thumbs his endless round of beads,
   Drawls out the dreary cadence of his creeds
And nods assent to each familiar line.

But she the goddess whose white star is set,
   Whose fane was pillaged for this sombre shrine,
   Could she look down upon those lips of thine,
And hear thee mutter, would she still regret?

There came a sound of singing on my ear,
   And slowly glided through the far-off door,
   A glimmer of grey forms like ghosts, they bore
A dead man lying on his purple bier.

Some poor man's soul, so little candle smoke
   Went curling upwards by the uncased shroud,
   And then a sudden thunder-clap broke loud,
And drowned the droning of the priest who spoke.

So all the shuffling feet passed out again
  To lightnings flashing through the wet and wind,
  And while I lingered in the gate behind
The dead man travelled through the storm and rain.

Rome, 1881.

AT LANUVIUM.

" Festo quid potius die
Neptuni faciam."
HORACE, *Odes*, iii. 28.

SPRING grew to perfect summer in one day,
     And we lay there among the vines, to gaze
Where Circe's isle floats purple, far away
     Above the golden haze :

And on our ears there seemed to rise and fall
     The burden of an old world song we knew,
That sang, " To-day is Neptune's festival,
     And we, what shall we do ?"

Go down brown-armed Campagna maid of mine,
     And bring again the earthern jar that lies
With three years' dust above the mellow wine ;
     And while the swift day dies,

You first shall sing a song of waters blue,
     Paphos and Cnidos in the summer seas,
And one who guides her swan-drawn chariot through
     The white-shored Cyclades ;

And I will take the second turn of song,
　Of floating tresses in the foam and surge
Where Nereid maids about the sea-god throng;
　And night shall have her dirge.

1881.

LUCCIOLE.

(To the author of "Pascarel.")

FOLLOW where the night-fire leads
　　Of the wingèd Lucciolá,
Where through waving river weeds
Water mirrors wreathed in reeds
　　Catch its glimmer from afar ;

Where the falling water plays,
　　Up the hillside, higher, higher,
In the pathless forest ways
Every branch is in a blaze,
　　With its tiny lamps of fire.

Are they fairies that have flown,
　　Stealing glamour from a star,
Flitting where wild weeds o'ergrown
Keep the forest all their own ?
　　Tell me of the Lucciolá.

Love they are as we to-night
　　In the branches tossed above ;

Only longing in their flight
That the moon and stars be bright,
　And the night be long for love.

Once the Love-God seemed to sorrow
　For the tears that he had cost ;
—Lending love to those who borrow,
But to lose him on the morrow ;—
　For the labour he had lost.

Fretting more that true love's sighs
　Go forgotten with the rest,　·
Fretting that his best work dies,
All the longing of the eyes,
　And the thrill from breast to breast.

He, of all good things the giver,
　Love, gave lovers this fair thing ;
That their vows should live for ever,
In the lights that glance and quiver,
　Through the summer night and spring ;

So that loves that rest unbroken
　Evermore recorded are,
Every word of passion spoken,
Every love-song has its token,
　Living in the Lucciolá.

1879.

"IF ANY ONE RETURN."

I WOULD we had carried him far away
    To the light of this south sun land,
Where the hills lean down to some red-rocked bay
And the sea's blue breaks into snow-white spray
    As the wave dies out on the sand.

Not there, not there, where the winds deface !
    Where the storm and the cloud race by !
But far away in this flowerful place
Where endless summers retouch, retrace,
    What flowers find heart to die.

And if ever the souls of the loved, set free,
    Come back to the souls that stay,
I could dream he would sit for awhile with me
Where I sit by this wonderful tideless sea
    And look to the red-rocked bay,

By the high cliff's edge where the wild weeds twine,
  And he would not speak or move,
But his eyes would gaze from his soul at mine,
My eyes that would answer without one sign,
  And that were enough for love.

And I think I should feel as the sun went round
  That he was not there any more,
But dews were wet on the grass-grown mound
On the bed of my love lying underground,
  And evening pale on the shore.

1879.

C

SONNETS.

"UNE HEURE VIENDRA QUI TOUT PAIERA."

IT was a tomb in Flanders, old and grey,
 A knight in armour, lying dead, unknown
Among the long-forgotten, yet the stone
Cried out for vengeance where the dead man lay;

No name was chiselled at his side to say
 What wrongs his spirit thirsted to atone,
 Only the armour with green moss o'ergrown,
And those grim words no years had worn away.

It may be haply in the songs of old
 His deeds were wonders to sweet music set,
 His name the thunder of a battle call,
Among the things forgotten and untold;
 His only record is the dead man's threat,—
 "An hour will come that shall atone for all!"

1879.

ALTHEA.

WHEN the last bitterness was past, shè bore
Her singing Cæsar to the Garden Hill,
Her fallen pitiful dead emperor.
She lifted up the beggar's cloak he wore
—The one thing living that he would not kill—
And on those lips of his that sang no more,
That world-loathed head which she found lovely still,
Her cold lips closed, in death she had her will.

Oh wreck of the lost human soul left free
To gorge the beast thy mask of manhood screened !
Because one living thing, albeit a slave,
Shed those hot tears on thy dishonoured grave,
Although thy curse be as the shoreless sea,
Because she loved, thou art not wholly fiend.

1881.

IMPERATOR AUGUSTUS.

IS this the man by whose decree abide
   The lives of countless nations, with the trace
  Of fresh tears wet upon the hard cold face?
—He wept, because a little child had died.

They set a marble image by his side,
   A sculptured Eros, ready for the chase ; .
  It wore the dead boy's features, and the grace
Of pretty ways that were the old man's pride.

And so he smiled, grown softer now, and tired
   Of too much empire, and it seemed a joy
Fondly to stroke and pet the curly head,
The smooth round limbs so strangely like the dead,
   To kiss the white lips of his marble boy
And call by name his little heart's-desired.

1879.

"ATQUE IN PERPETUUM FRATER AVE ATQUE VALE."

THIS was the end love made,—the hard-drawn breath,
    The last long sigh that ever man sighs here ;
And then for us, the great unanswered fear,
Will love live on,—the other side of death ?

Only a year and I had hoped to spend
    A life of pleasant communing, to be
    A kindred spirit holding fast to thee,
We never thought that love had such an end.

This was the end love made, for our delight,
    ` For one sweet year he cannot take away ;—
Those tapers burning in the dim half-light,
    Those kneeling women with a cross that pray,
And there, beneath green leaves and lilies white,
    Beyond the reach of love, our loved one lay.

1879.

SONGS.

Long After.

I SEE your white arms gliding,
   In music o'er the keys,
Long drooping lashes hiding
   A blue like summer seas ;
The sweet lips wide asunder,
   That tremble as you sing,
I could not choose but wonder,
   You seemed so fair a thing.

For all these long years after
   The dream has never died,
I still can hear your laughter,
   Still see you at my side ;
One lily hiding under
   The waves of golden hair ;
I could not choose but wonder,
   You were so strangely fair.

I keep the flower you braided
  Among those waves of gold,
The leaves are sere and faded,
  And like our love grown old.
Our lives have lain asunder,
  The years are long, and yet,
I could not choose but wonder,
  I cannot quite forget.

1880.

"Where the Rhone goes down to the Sea."

A SWEET still night of the vintage time,
    Where the Rhone goes down to the sea ;
The distant sound of a midnight chime
    Comes over the wave to me.
Only the hills and the stars o'erhead
Bring back dreams of the days long dead,
    While the Rhone goes down to the sea.

The years are long, and the world is wide,
    And we all went down to the sea ;
The ripples splash as we onward glide,
    And I dream they are here with me—
All lost friends whom we all loved so,
In the old mad life of long ago,
    Who all went down to the sea.

So we passed in the golden days
　With the summer down to the sea.
They wander still over weary ways,
　And come not again to me.
I am here alone with the night wind's sigh,
The fading stars, and a dream gone by,
　And the Rhone going down to the sea.

1880.

MAIDENHAIR.

I REMEMBER low on the water
  They hung from the dripping moss
In the broken shrine of some stream-god's daughter,
  Where the North and the South roads cross.
And I plucked some sprays for my love to wear,
Some tangled sprays of the maidenhair.

So you went North with the swallow,
  Away from this Southern shore,
And the summers pass, and the winters follow,
  And the years, but you come no more.—
You have roses now in your breast to wear,
And you have forgotten the maidenhair.

And the sound of echoing laughter
  The songs that we used to sing,
To remember these in the days long after,
  May seem but a foolish thing.
Yet I know to me they are always fair,
My withered sprays of the maidenhair.

1879.

A Song of Autumn.

A LL through the golden weather
    Until the autumn fell,
Our lives went by together
    So wildly and so well.—

But autumn's wind uncloses
    The heart of all your flowers,
I think as with the roses,
    So hath it been with ours.

Like some divided river
    Your ways and mine will be,
—To drift apart for ever,
    For ever till the sea.

And yet, for one word spoken,
    One whisper of regret,
The dream had not been broken
    And love were with us yet.

1880.

D

ATALANTA.

WAIT not along the shore, they will not come ;
    The suns go down beyond the windy seas,
Those weary sails shall never wing them home
      O'er this white foam ;
      No voice from these
On any landward wind that dies among the trees.

Gone south, it may be, rudderless, astray,
Gone where the winds and ocean currents bore,
Out of all tracks along the sea's highway
      This many a day,
      To some far shore
Where never wild seas break, or any fierce winds roar.

For there are lands ye never recked of yet
Between the blue of stormless sea and sky,
Beyond where any suns of yours have set,
      Or these waves fret ;
      And loud winds die
In cloudless summertide, where those far islands lie.

They will not come ! for on the coral shore
The good ship lies, by little waves caressed,
All stormy ways and wanderings are o'er,
        No more, no more !
        But long sweet rest,
In cool green meadow-lands, that lie along the West.

Or if beneath far fathom depths of waves
She lies heeled over by the slow tide's sweep,
Deep down where never any swift sea raves,
        Through ocean caves,
        A dreaming deep
Of softly gliding forms, a glimmering world of sleep.

Then have they passed beyond the outer gate
Through death to knowledge of all things, and so
From out the silence of their unknown fate
        They bid us wait,
        Who only know
That twixt their loves and ours the great seas ebb and
    flow.

1880.

"WHEN I AM DEAD."

WHEN I am dead, my spirit
   Shall wander far and free,
Through realms the dead inherit
   Of earth and sky and sea ;
Through morning dawn and gloaming,
   By midnight moons at will,
By shores where the waves are foaming,
   By seas where the waves are still.
I following late behind you,
   In wingless sleepless flight,
Will wander till I find you,
   In sunshine or twilight ;
With silent kiss for greeting
   On lips and eyes and head,
In that strange after-meeting
   Shall love be perfected.
We shall lie in summer breezes
   And pass where whirlwinds go,
And the Northern blast that freezes
   Shall bear us with the snow.

We shall stand above the thunder,
    And watch the lightnings hurled
At the misty mountains under,
    Of the dim forsaken world.
We shall find our footsteps' traces,
    And passing hand in hand
By old familiar places,
    We shall laugh, and understand.

1881.

"THOSE DAYS ARE LONG DEPARTED."

THOSE days are long departed,
　　Gone where the dead dreams are,
Since we two children started
　　To look for the morning star.

We asked our way of the swallow
　　In his language that we knew,
We were sad we could not follow
　　So swift the blue bird flew.

We set our wherry drifting
　　Between the poplar trees,
And the banks of meadows shifting
　　Were the shores of unknown seas.

We talked of the white snow prairies
　　That lie by the Northern lights,
And of woodlands where the fairies
　　Are seen in the moonlit nights.

Till one long day was over
   And we grew too tired to roam,
And through the corn and clover
   We slowly wandered home.

Ah child ! with love and laughter
   We had journeyed out so far;
We who went in the big years after
   To look for another star ;

But I go unbefriended
   Through wind and rain and foam,—
One day was hardly ended
   When the angel took you home.

1881.

AFTER HEINE.

HOW the mirrored moonbeams quiver
　On the waters' fall and rise,
Yet the moon serene as ever
　Wanders through the quiet skies.

Like the mirrored moonlight's fretting
　Are the dreams I have of you,
For my heart will beat, forgetting
　You are ever calm and true.

ENDYMION.

S HE came upon me in the middle day,
    Bowed o'er the waters of a mountain mere ;
Where dimly mirrored in the ripple's play
        I saw some fair thing near.

I saw the waters lapping round her feet,
    The widening rings spread, follow out and die,
I saw the mirror and the mirrored meet,
        And heard a voice hard by.

So I, Endymion, who lay bathing there,
    Half-hidden in the coolness of the lake,
Looked up and swept away my long wild hair,
        And knew a goddess spake ;

A form white limbed and peerless, far above
    The very fairest of imagined things,
The perfect vision of a dream of love
        Stepped through the water-rings ;

That breathed soft names and drew me to her arms,
　White arms and clinging in a long caress,
And won me willing, by the magic charms
　　Of perfect loveliness :

Till on my breast a throbbing bosom lies ;
　The dim hills waver and the dark woods roll,
For all the longing of two glorious eyes
　　Takes hold upon my soul.

Then only when the sudden darkness fell
　Upon the silver of the mountain mere,
And through the pine trees of the slanting dell,
　　The moon rose cold and clear.

I seemed alone upon the dewy shore,—
　For she had left me as she came unwarned ;—
And fell from sighing into sleep, before
　　The summer morning dawned.

What wonder now I find no maiden fair
　Who dwells between these mountains and the seas?
And go unloving and unloved, or ere
　　I turn to such as these.

What wonder if the light of those wide eyes
　Makes other eyes seem cold ; for that loud laughter
Lost love have nothing left but sighs
　　For all the time hereafter.

Yet better so, far better, no regret
　　Can touch my heart for that sweet memory's sake,
But only sighing for the sun that set
　　　　Behind the summer lake.

*　　　*　　　*　　　*　　　*

But yestermorn it was, the second night
　　Comes softly stealing over yon blue steep ;
The world grows silent in the fading light,
　　　　There is no joy but sleep.

—I cannot bear her fair face in the skies
　　Beyond the drowsy waving of the trees,—
A soft breeze kisses round my heavy eyes,
　　　　A restful summer breeze.

What means this dreamless apathy of sleep?
　　—A mist steals over the dim lake, the shore,
Until my closing eyes forget to weep—
　　　　Oh, let me wake no more !

DISILLUSION.

A H ! what would youth be doing
   To hoist his crimson sails,
To leave the wood-doves cooing,
  The song of nightingales ;
To leave this woodland quiet
  For murmuring winds at strife,
For waves that foam and riot
  About the seas of life.

From still bays silver sanded
  Wild currents hasten down,
To rocks where ships are stranded
  And eddies where men drown.
Far out, by hills surrounded,
  Is the golden haven gate,
And all beyond unbounded
  Are shoreless seas of fate.

They steer for those far highlands
    Across the summer tide,
And dream of fairy islands
    Upon the further side.
They only see the sunlight,
    The flashing of gold bars,
But the other side is moonlight
    And glimmer of pale stars.

They will not heed the warning
    Blown back on every wind,
For hope is born with morning,
    The secret is behind.
Whirled through in wild confusion
    They pass the narrow strait,
To the sea of disillusion
    That lies beyond the gate.

REQUIESCAT.

H E had the poet's eyes,
    —Sing to him sleeping,—
Sweet grace of low replies,
    —Why are we weeping?—

He had the gentle ways,
    —Fair dreams befall him !—
Beauty through all his days,
    —Then why recall him ?—

That which in him was fair
    Still shall be ours :
Yet, yet my heart lies there
    Under the flowers.

1881.

www.ingramcontent.com/pod-product-compliance
Lightning Source LLC
Chambersburg PA
CBHW022155020726
47496CB00008B/2723